The Lighthouse Keeper Tales

The Lighthouse Keeper's Tea first published in 2001 by Scholastic Ltd
The Lighthouse Keeper's Breakfast first published in 2000 by Scholastic Ltd
This edition first published in 2009 by Scholastic Children's Books
Euston House, 24 Eversholt Street
London NW1 1DB
a division of Scholastic Ltd
www.scholastic.co.uk
London ~ New York ~ Toronto ~ Sydney ~ Auckland
Mexico City ~ New Delhi ~ Hong Kong

1 3 5 7 9 10 8 6 4 2

The Lighthouse Keeper's Breakfast

Mr and Mrs Grinling lived with their cat, Hamish, in a little white cottage perched high on the cliffs. Mr Grinling was a lighthouse keeper. By day and night, with his assistant Sam, he lovingly tended the light.

One Wednesday morning when Sam was polishing, he noticed a tiny inscription right at the top of the lighthouse.

"Well, well," he said to himself. "Just fancy that!"

"Our lighthouse is 200 years old this year," he told everyone. "We should celebrate."

"Maybe some presents," said Mr Grinling. "And a fresh coat of red and white paint."

"And a party," said Mrs Grinling.

"How about fancy dress?" suggested Sally de la Croissant, the baker.

"Something to do with the sea," said Jason the postman. "I've got a lovely octopus suit."

NOTICE BOARD

THE LIGHTHOUSE
BIRTHDAY CELEBRATION
200 YEARS OLD

• VERY SPECIAL GUESTS: MR + MRS GRINLING
• ALL NIGHT SEA PARTY FOLLOWED BY
  A BIRTHDAY BREAKFAST
• *PLEASE WEAR FANCY DRESS*

RSVP: SALLY DE LA
CROISSANT

"We can use my old sailing ship," roared Admiral Fleetabix, "I'll moor her out in the bay."

"Can it be an all night party with a birthday breakfast?" asked the children. "It is an extremely important occasion."

And everyone agreed that Mr and Mrs Grinling should be the Very Special Guests.

 It was so difficult to choose the best fancy dress costume.

"Shall I wear the shark suit?" asked Mr Grinling.

"Could I be a mermaid?" wondered Mrs Grinling.

But then they discovered the pirate costumes.

"All my life I've yearned to be a pirate," sighed Mrs Grinling. "To spit and swear and roam the seven seas."

"And search for treasure," added Mr Grinling.

"We'll be splendid pirates!" cried Mrs Grinling as she swashed and buckled around the room.

"Oo-aargh!" said Mr Grinling and he swashed and buckled too.

"Perhaps Hamish could be our pirate cat," suggested Mrs Grinling. But Hamish had very different ideas. Whenever Mrs Grinling wanted him to try his pirate costume, Hamish disappeared.

"Drat that cat," she exclaimed. "Where does he go these days?"

The Grinlings practised being pirates at every opportunity.

But Mr Grinling's cutlass caused all sorts of difficulties.

"I do want to be a pirate," he said sadly. "I'm just not very good at it. Perhaps I should have gone as a shark after all."

Mrs Grinling quite frightened
Sam and the seagulls with her
cursing and swearing.

On the night of the party the Grinlings rowed out towards the party ship. At first its lights shone clearly across the water but gradually they dimmed and soon they vanished altogether.

"What can have happened, Mrs G?" said Mr Grinling. "We can't be lost." The waves slapped against the little boat. It was darker than Mr Grinling had ever seen it. And then as the lighthouse flashed across the bay…

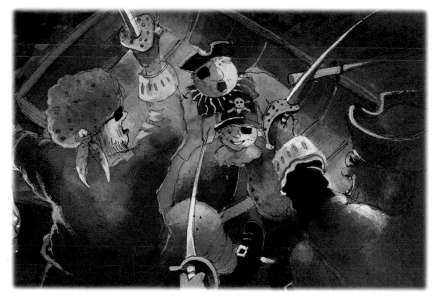

"Look, Mr G!" exclaimed
Mrs Grinling. "Someone to
rescue us."

A speed boat swished in beside
them and three pirates leapt
across the bow, thrusting their
shining cutlasses in the air.

"Oo-aargh!" they roared and
they rampaged round the dinghy.

Mrs Grinling was delighted.

"Real pirates," she whispered
to Mr Grinling and she forgot all
about the Sea Party.

"Oo-aargh," growled the fiercest
pirate. "We be pirates and this
be our pirate patch. We're on the
look-out for likely new recruits."

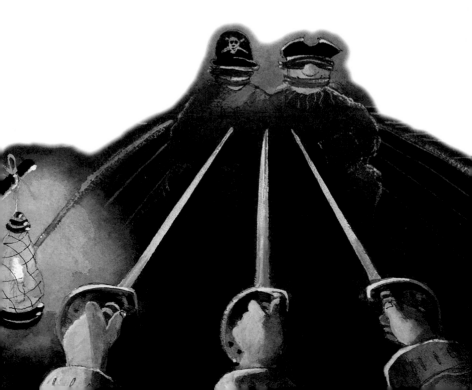

"Oh, yes please!" exclaimed Mrs Grinling. "We'd love to be pirates. Yo-ho-ho and a bottle of rum."

Mr Grinling waved his cutlass rather feebly. The pirates appeared rather surprised.

"First you have to pass the Incredibly Difficult Pirate Tests," snarled the smallest and smelliest pirate. Mr Grinling wasn't sure about pirate tests.

"We'll blindfold 'em and take 'em back to the Captain," shouted the fiercest pirate. "She'll soon find out if they're made of proper pirate material."

The pirate captain was a particularly nasty-looking piece of work. She had black teeth and smelt of rotten fish and seaweed. A grubby white parrot clung to her shoulder.

"Right, me hearties, what have we 'ere?" She peg-legged around the Grinlings. "So you want to join our pirate crew?"

"Yes, please," said Mrs Grinling.

"Definitely," agreed Mr Grinling.

"Well, you look like pirates and you smell like pirates, but you have to pass the six pirate tests before you can be pirates. Are you ready?" asked the Captain. "So what comes first, me hearties?"

"The Swearing Test!" shouted the pirates.

Mrs Grinling swore loud and long. The parrot covered his ears. Mr Grinling thought for a while.

"Blithering bumbollards," he muttered at last. The pirates shook their heads.

"Now the Sleeping in a Hammock in a Force Nine Gale Test. Rock that ship, me bully boys and girls."

Mrs Grinling held tightly to the hammock sides and smiled happily. Mr Grinling bounced right out of his hammock and was seasick several times.

The pirates groaned.

"The Jolly Roger Flag Test," shouted Captain Bosibelle. "Just a quick climb to the crow's-nest."

Mrs Grinling scampered up the rope ladder. At the top she not only hoisted the flag but waved her cutlass.

"Shiver me timbers!" shouted the pirates.

Mr Grinling closed his eyes as he started to climb.

"Don't look down," he muttered to himself. "Think of Hamish and Sam. Think of nice things to eat, Peach Surprise and iced sea biscuits, think of-ah-ah-ah…"

He fell into a barrel of foul-smelling water.

"I'm so sorry," said the Captain.

"They're very polite for pirates, Mrs G," spluttered Mr Grinling.

"Pirate Test number four," announced Captain Bosibelle.

"Finding the Treasure," roared all the pirates.

"Here's the map," said Captain Bosibelle. "There's lovely treasure hidden on our ship, you've got ten minutes to find it."

"Oo-aargh," shouted the Grinlings. They found the treasure chest under the bottom of a very small pirate. It contained only one jewel and two pieces of eight.

"We're a little short of treasure at the moment," explained the Captain. "No decent raids lately.

"And now the most dangerous, the most terrifying, the most dastardly test of them all."

"Eating Pirate Food!" shouted the pirates.

"Eating," said Mr Grinling happily. "Now eating is something I can do." Some of the smaller pirates sniggered. Captain Bosibelle laid out the food. Two maggots and a weevil wriggled across the biscuit. Mrs Grinling turned quite green but Mr Grinling ate it, weevils, maggots and all.

"Hurrah!" cheered the pirates.

"And now number six, the final test," roared the Captain. "If you pass this you can join our pirate gang. Tell 'em, me bouncing buccaneers."

"Walking the Plank," cried the pirates.

"Oh," said Mrs Grinling.

"Dearie me," said Mr Grinling.

The water below looked
smoothly dark and menacing.
Mr Grinling wished he was
wearing the shark costume.

"Do you think I could ask for
arm bands?" he whispered.
Mrs Grinling looked at the
pirates' faces and shook her head.

"We've always wanted to be pirates, Mr G," she said. "We aren't afraid of a little bit of water, are we?"

"Goodness, no," said Mr Grinling. But his knees knocked and his tummy felt all wobbly like a jelly.

"Ready," he said and he held his nose.

"Steady," said Mrs Grinling and she closed her eyes.

"Just a minute," said Mr Grinling, letting go of his nose. "Something's amiss here. Whoever heard of new pirates walking the plank? We could drown before we've done any pirating."

Suddenly the pirates pulled off their disguises.

"Surprise!" they shouted. The Grinlings were astounded.

"Jason the postman!" exclaimed Mr Grinling.

"Admiral Fleetabix!" cried Mrs Grinling.

"And Sally de la Croissant!" they said both together.

"We heard how you longed to be pirates," she explained. "So we planned a Pirate Experience. We had to be nasty so you'd think we were real."

"We certainly did," said Mr Grinling as he mopped his brow.

The lighthouse beamed its last light across the bay.

"It's party time," called Jason, picking up his fiddle.

"May I have the pleasure, Pirate Herbert?" asked Mrs Grinling.

"Oo-aargh, Pirate Hattie!" smiled Mr Grinling.

And they all danced until they could dance no more.

"Sun's up!" called Sally de la Croissant. "Time for the birthday breakfast."

Mrs Grinling looked worried.

"We can't have the party without Hamish."

"Or Sam," said Mr Grinling.

"They're coming, they're coming!" shouted the children.

"Just in time for the food," said Sam as he climbed on to the deck. He placed a large, wicker basket at the Grinlings' feet and carefully opened the lid. Out jumped…

Hamish and Mrs Hamish and four little Hamishes.

"Now that's what I call real treasure," smiled Mr Grinling.

The Lighthouse Keeper's Tea

Mr and Mrs Grinling lived with their cat, Hamish, and his family in a little white house perched high on a cliff. Some days Mr Grinling was the lighthouse keeper, but other days he just got in Mrs Grinling's way.

"Mr G, Mr G, you're always under my feet," complained Mrs Grinling.

Mr Grinling sighed.

"I'm bored, Mrs G. Now that Sam helps at the lighthouse, I haven't got enough to do."

"A new pastime," replied Mrs Grinling, "that's what you need. What do you enjoy doing?"

"Eating?" suggested
Mr Grinling. He dipped his
finger in the icing. "That's it,"
he said, "the perfect pastime.
If I like eating I'm sure I'd
like cooking."

Mrs Grinling looked alarmed.

"Perhaps I could help?"

"No thank you," said
Mr Grinling. "I can do it myself.
You have a little rest while I make
some bread for our lunch. Just pop
in these ingredients,
mix them about a bit
and hey presto, the
bread will be ready
in no time."

The bread rose and rose and…

…flopped. When Mr Grinling
tried to put it in the oven the
dough slithered
everywhere.

"I don't like
cooking," he
decided. "Much
too messy."

"Oh dear, such a pity," said Mrs Grinling. "Perhaps something outdoors would suit you better. What about birdwatching with your telescope?"

"Good idea, Mrs G," agreed Mr Grinling. "I could keep an eye on those pesky seagulls."

So he packed a little something and set out.

"Here's your warm jumper," Mrs Grinling called after him.

"No, thank you," replied Mr Grinling. "It's a beautiful day, look at that sun."

He didn't see any seagulls, but he did spy: five greenfinches, four mistle thrushes...

...three mallard ducks, two black swans...

and a kingfisher on the river bank. 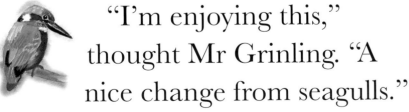 "I'm enjoying this," thought Mr Grinling. "A nice change from seagulls." It was during lunch that he remembered that he didn't like...

…cows.

"Shoo," he said bravely.

"Moo," mooed the gentle cows.

Mr Grinling scrambled up
the tree while the cows finished
his cheese, lettuce and tomato
sandwiches. He rang Sam.

"Help, help, I'm sure I've just
seen a dangerous wild boar."

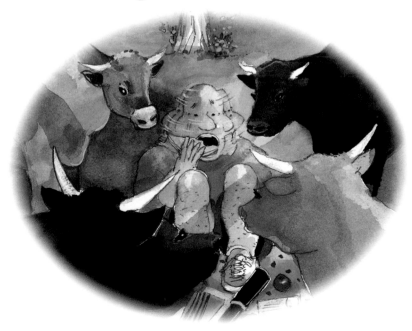

Sam was surprised. "A wild boar?"

"Ferocious," said Mr Grinling. "And I'm very cold. Please rescue me."

"Where are you?" asked Sam.

"Well," explained Mr Grinling. "I'm up a very thin tree, in a field, surrounded by a green hedge and a few cows."

It took Sam several hours to find him.

"No more birdwatching," said Mr Grinling. "Far too dangerous with all those wild…"

"Cows?" said Sam helpfully.

But Mr Grinling was still bored.

"Oh dear," he thought. "There must be something I enjoy."

 He tried the violin, but that was too screechy for everyone. He went out with his kite, but that was too windy. And then there was the roller blading, but that was an absolute disaster.

"Perhaps old dogs can't learn new tricks," teased Mrs Grinling.

"Old!" spluttered Mr Grinling. "Did you say old? Sea dogs like me are never too old to learn new tricks. I just haven't found the perfect one yet."

"M-m-m," said Mrs Grinling.

 One morning in Wild Horses Bay, Mr Grinling met Sam carrying a large board. He was surprised.

"I didn't know you were a surfer, Sam."

"One of the best," boasted Sam, and he rode the big waves while Mr Grinling watched.

"I wish I could do that," said Mr Grinling.

"Come and have a go," called Sam. He pulled Mr Grinling onto the surfboard.

"There might be a bit of a problem," said Mr Grinling.

But Sam didn't hear him.
Mr Grinling stood up on the
surfboard…and he fell off
the surfboard.

"Swim!" shouted Sam.

"Glug, glug," glugged
Mr Grinling. "I can't," he
spluttered. "That's the bit of
a problem."

"Uh-uh," Sam shook his head.
"If you want to be a surfer, that's
not a bit of a problem, that's an
enormous problem."

"I'm an extremely good floater," said Mr Grinling hopefully.

But Sam was firm.

"If you can't swim, you can't be a surfer."

But Mr Grinling had made up his mind. Surfing was what he wanted to do most in the world.

"Don't breathe a word to Mrs G," said Mr Grinling. "She thinks old dogs can't learn new tricks. I'll show her that this one can."

"Shall I help you with the swimming?" asked Sam.

"No, thank you," said Mr Grinling. "I know exactly what to do."

He found a rock in just the right place and lowered himself into the water.

"I splash with my arms like this, and kick with my feet like this! And then I do both together…"

"Glug, glug," glugged Mr Grinling, splashing wildly. "Help, help," cried Mr Grinling, "I'm drowning!"

"Lucky I'm such a good floater," remembered Mr Grinling, turning over.

He floated around the old jetty and through the Needles. He floated beside the white sand beach and over the wreck of the *Hesperus*. He floated across the channel rippling with irritable little waves.

He floated past the lighthouse
and the little white house.
    At last he floated up onto
the beach.

"Perhaps I do need a little bit of
help," he whispered to Hamish as
he crept to bed.

"JOIN TODAY"
said the notice at
the Green Lagoon Pool.

GREEN LAGOON
• Beginner's Class •

"I've come to learn to swim,"
said Mr Grinling.

"We've got just the class for
you," replied the swimming
instructor. "First we'll try
the kicking."

"Glug, glug," glugged
Mr Grinling and he sank to
the bottom of the pool.

"Now we'll use our arms," called the instructor.

"Splash, splash," splashed Mr Grinling, but he still sank. The children watched.

"We'll help you, Mr Grinling," they said. And they did.

Soon he could dog paddle, freestyle, backstroke and butterfly.

"Congratulations," said the swimming instructor. "I always say you're never too old to learn."

"Well done!" exclaimed Sam. "Now I'll show you how to surf."

"No, thank you," said Mr Grinling. "I'll do it myself."

"Stubborn old sea dog," said Sam quietly.

Mr Grinling bought a bright yellow wetsuit and a shiny red surfboard. Every day he practised where he thought no one could see him and every day he fell into the water hundreds of times.

"One thousand and one," muttered Mr Grinling as he scrambled onto the board again.

"This time I'll do it," he called to the seagulls.

"I think he needs a helping hand," said Sam to the children. "Are you ready for action?"

Seven shark fins rose in the water.
"Blither my whiskers!" shouted
Mr Grinling.

Seven sharks surfed beside
him. Mr Grinling stayed on
the surfboard all the way to
the shallows.

Seven sharks climbed out of the water.

"Well," cried Sam, "our shark trick certainly helped an old sea dog learn his new trick!"

"You frightened the life out of me," said Mr Grinling, but a grin stretched right across his face.

It wasn't long before Mr Grinling could ride the waves just like a real surfer.

"Now I can show Mrs Grinling," he announced.

"Not yet, not yet," begged the children. "We've thought of the perfect occasion."

 On the day of the
Wild Horse Bay
Sea Carnival,
Mrs Grinling
searched high and
low for Mr Grinling.

"I don't understand. He always
enters the sandcastle competition
and runs in the sack race.
Whatever's happened to him?
Wherever can he be?" she asked
the children.

"Don't worry," they said, and
they arranged a deck chair for her.
"So you can get a better view of the
surfing," they explained. And they
all lined up at the water's edge.

As the big wave rose up across
the bay, the drums began to roll.
Mrs Grinling watched the little
round figure on the surfboard.

"Such daring!" she exclaimed.

"Amazing!" she cheered.

"Extraordinary!" she gasped.

The figure in yellow surfed almost to her feet. He peeled off his wetsuit and bowed.

"I'd like you to meet an old sea dog," he said. Mrs Grinling was speechless. She gave Mr Grinling a great big hug.

"I did it all by myself," he said proudly. "With a little bit of help from Sam and the children."

"In that case," said Mrs Grinling, "I think we should have a splendiferous surfing tea."

"We'll help if you like," said the children.

And they did.